Jacob Yost

Incubators and Brooders

How to build and successfully manage them

Jacob Yost

Incubators and Brooders
How to build and successfully manage them

ISBN/EAN: 9783337380762

Printed in Europe, USA, Canada, Australia, Japan

Cover: Foto ©Andreas Hilbeck / pixelio.de

More available books at **www.hansebooks.com**

INCUBATORS AND BROODERS.

How to Build and Successfully Manage them.

The Care, Cure and Protection

——OF——

POULTRY.

How to Build up the Quality of the Flock.

The kind of a House to Build; How to Build it,

——AND——

OTHER USEFUL INFORMATION.

BY JACOB YOST

ARKANSAS CITY, KANSAS.
COPYRIGHTED, 1895.

Introductory.

In putting out this book I have kept in mind those to whom it will be of most benefit. I have had ten years experience in the raising of poultry and if that experience is worth anything to those interested in the business I will feel that I have done well in imparting desirable information as well as gaining a profit to myself.

The description of the machines and buildings are carried out minutely so that the boys and girls can read them intelligently and by the assistance of the materials and a few tools they will find all the information necessary to carry out everything essential to a successful end.

THE AUTHOR.

The Hen as a Money-maker.

The hen converts grass into greenbacks, grain into gold and for the sand and gravel she returns us silver. No other animal on the farm can compare with her. The horse and cow are heavy consumers and with the best economy are more or less costly. The hen yields the farmer more for the investment than any other animal, and gives him the least trouble. She asks nothing of him unless he chooses to give it to her, but if he so chooses to supply her needs, she returns the compliment many fold and places at his disposal an article which is demanded in his domestic economy. The egg is converted into many uses. Its utility is so general that we often lose sight of its importance and fail to give the hen the great credit that is due her. The housewife has need of the egg in

many ways and without it her table would be
set with a limited variety. She must have eggs
at all times of the year and at whatever cost.
In her mind the poultry yard is an essential
annex to the kitchen, and from it comes many
delicate dishes that cannot be replaced by viands
from any other source. The egg has its place
among remedial agents, and in this department
has gained for itself no insignificant reputation.
Like the song birds the hen is found wherever
man sees fit to make his habitation, and how-
ever distant in the frontier he may advance the
hen is found as his companion. But unlike the
song bird the hen, although possessed of wings,
stays with him the year round, and when nature
fails to give him food she places herself at his
service and helps to sustain him. She asks but
little of him for her kindness. The waste from
his table is often all that is required. With this
she constitutes herself an establishment more
valued than the mint, because she helps to provide his essential needs. She is thoroughly a
domestic animal, and to do her part in the
domestic economy of the home, she must have
protection and attention.

As an investment for profit the hen must be
made to lay eggs in winter as well as in spring

and summer. To have her do this she must be provided with those comforts that will place her in the proper condition for this service. These are healthy and comfortable quarters and good food. When a hen has to get out in a snow storm for food or go without, is it any wonder that she does not lay during such weather? Yet many farmers wonder why they don't have eggs to sell when there is a good market for them. Hens will lay in winter time if they are surrounded with the conditions that fit them for it. It is important to have good layers, yet there is not as much importance attached to that fact as there is that they be properly treated. Different breeds of chickens are noted for different qualities. Attention paid to the treatment of any breed is productive of more eggs than in the choice of a breed noted for laying. In feeding hens in winter give them as many of the summer dishes as you can command, such as gravel, dust baths, greens of different kinds, fresh water not ice cold, meats, ground bone, charcoal and grits of different kinds.

By the use of an incubator chickens can be hatched at any time of the year, and if the best market is in view, bring the chickens off in February and March. The best time to get an incubator and a brooder is in the fall. My experience proves to me that chickens hatched in an incubator and cared for in a brooder from the middle of September till the middle of November, will in this latitude feather out sufficiently before cold weather sets in, and be ready to go into the best market of the year as broilers. It is a known fact that with a brooder you can raise 90 per cent. of the chickens hatched while the hen raises but 50 per cent. of her brood. Then why bother with an old setting hen when the brooder will doubly discount her and be of less trouble? It is also a known fact that the setting hens breed mites, lice and other vermin and are the means of infecting the whole flock, while the incubator does not give a chance for vermin of any kind to infect its household. It will require fifteen hens to hatch the same number of eggs as an incubator of 200 egg capacity. These fifteen hens can be made to lay during the three weeks hatching time. While the incubator does the hatching the value of the eggs layed during this time will doubly pay for the oil used in running the incubator. After the hens have brought off their chickens they run with them from six to eight weeks, a period of time which is unprofitable and wholly wasted. The care of the incubator and brooder combined is not nearly so much as the care of the hens and their individual broods. With good eggs and proper care two hatchings by the incubator will pay for it and also the brooder. Your investment is then back and you have the appliances that will be serviceable for years, to carry on a business that calls for a very small expense.

The Selection of Good Layers.

Do not keep any chickens that appear stunted. They always degrade the appearance of a flock. When once a fowl becomes stunted it is not fit for breeding purposes, and in fact is not worth the keeping. Disease or a tendency towards disease is hereditary. Discard all hens that have a tendency to lay on fat, and retain those that under proper feeding will convert the food into eggs instead of fat. If part of the flock convert the food into fat instead of eggs, the profit is consumed by the drones. No fowl should be retained that does not in some manner add to the profit of the flock. Much care should be exercised in selecting layers for breeding purposes every year, and in a short time the entire flock will consist of nothing else but layers.   A good layer has a small head a long neck and back, and a wedge shaped body.   The eyes are bright and the comb and wattles are of a bright red, she is energetic and active, starting at every sound or motion with an elastic spring.   A good layer always lays eggs that will hatch well.   The very fact that she is a good layer shows that she is in a healthy condition.   The result of good laying is the greater number of the eggs are fertile, and the chickens will be strong and vigorous.   A hen is profitable until she is three years old.   After that the number of eggs she lays will decrease.   She should not be kept longer unless she is a "world beater," and is perfectly healthy.   The hens that moult early should be kept in preference to those that moult late.   They will come into profit early in winter when eggs are yet a good price.

WHY DO HENS STOP LAYING IN COLD WEATHER.

The most profitable hens are those which lay at a time when eggs are scarce and consequently dear.   The thing to do is to provide conditions that will induce hens to lay at the desired time.   Laying hens depend less upon the seasons

than they do upon the weather. This being
the case all poultry keepers should provide comfortable quarters for all kinds of inclement
weather, both winter and summer. It is often
the case that hens are in good condition and are
laying regularly. When the first cold spell
comes they suddenly stop laying. This is a
matter that is worthy the attention of those
interested in poultry and also has its effect upon
the consumer. It is a question of no small
concern when eggs are worth three cents a piece
to have the hens suddenly quit business. At this
time it is most desirable to have them continue
filling the egg basket and if necessary take
their vacation at some other time when eggs
are cheaper and the market is full. It seems
strange after continuing to lay with due regu-
larity for an indefinite period and when eggs
are plentiful to stop because the price has
advanced. There are causes for all this that
are not real. It is not for lack of food as they
often stop laying in a single day. It is not due
to disease as the hens may be perfectly healthy
at such a time. The true cause is for the lack
of warmth. The heat of body comes by the
digestion of food, and when they are exposed
to the cold or inclement weather there is not

enough of heat generated by their food to protect them sufficiently.   Egg production ceases under these conditions, because all the vitality of the hen is required in protection from the cold.

The remedy for this is to protect against the loss of animal heat.   Hence there must be shelter from the cold and additional comforts to keep the conditions as the egg laying business requires.

How to Prepare For Winter.

Every one concerned in raising poultry should be fully interested in this part of the business. Many persons called breeders of poultry are not deserving of the name.   Too often do we see rickety quarters for the chickens that would not serve as a protection from a hail stone, much less from a rain, wind storm or the snows of winter.   Besides being rickety it is often found badly located, unclean and full of vermin, and yet the chickens are expected to maintain this as their quarters and put sheckles into pockets of their lord and master who so generously allows them an existence and a living under such shameful conditions.   It would be a credit to such persons to kill off their poultry as an act of charity, burn down the house and go out of the business. If this is the condition of your chicken house, dear reader, don't let another day pass until you have set about providing better and more comfortable quarters for the bird that has been provided for you, and which serves you in a manner that deserves your best efforts and most devoted attention. Build a good double wall chicken house, well ventilated, with shed on south side, with plenty of glass for light and sunshine for their winter quarters. After providing comfortable quarters feed them warm food in the mornings. Throw fine grain in among some straw to keep them working during the day. When the weather is cold never let them drink ice cold water. Always empty the drinking vessels in the evening and never give them water in the morning until they have had their morning feed. Don't let the cold air enter the ventilators, cracks or other openings in stormy weather. If you wish the hens to lay in winter as they do in summer provide similar conditions, and they will do the work to your satisfaction. If the poultry is placed in these conditions they will amply repay for all trouble, and be a source of profit and pleasure to their owner.

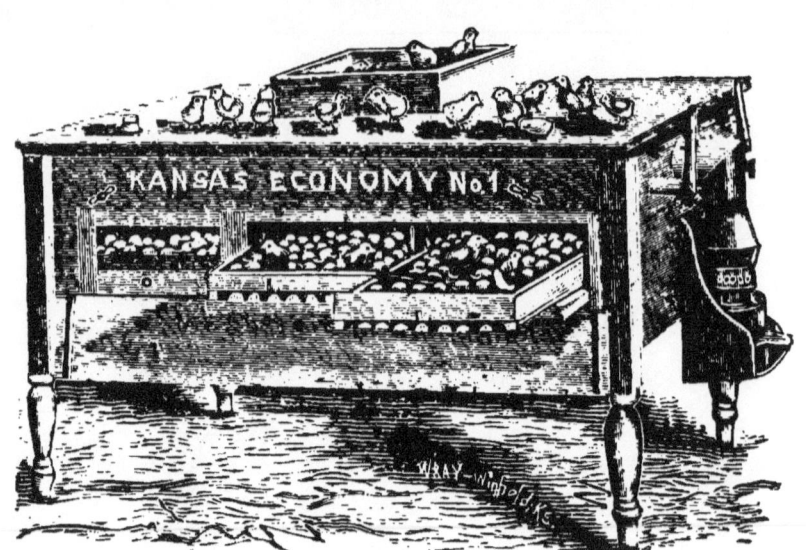

How to Make Incubator No. 1.

CAPACITY 300 EGGS.

An incubator is made up essentially of four parts and is built in the order here named. A ventilator, an egg chamber, a hot water tank, and the outer cabinet enclosing these parts. Use $7/8$ inch lumber, unless otherwise mentioned. Make a frame with front piece $3\frac{3}{4}$ inches wide by 4 feet 9 inches long, back piece $3\frac{1}{4}$ inches wide by 4 feet 7 7-16 inches long, end pieces $3\frac{3}{8}$ inches by 2 feet 11 inches long. Nail front pieces on ends, put back piece between ends, making distance between front and back pieces 2 feet $6\frac{5}{8}$ inches, corners square. Cover bottom with 1x6 flooring cut 5 feet 4 inches long, making ends project $3\frac{1}{2}$ inches. Draw crosswise two lines dividing space enclosed by frame into three equal parts, and one line lengthwise midway between front and back. In center of each square bore a $3/4$ inch hole and cover each hole with a block 1 inch thick and 3 or 4 inches square, and nail fast. Cut 4 pieces 1 inch by 1 inch by 2 feet 65/8 inces long. Place one in each end and one on each mark drawn across the floor. Fill in with saw-dust, level with the 1 inch pieces. Cover this again with ½ inch lumber and nail it securely. Bore the holes on through the pieces last put on. Cover the last floor with building paper and fasten with 4 oz. tacks. In each hole put a tin tube from the upper side. Make 24 pieces ½ inch by ¾ inch by 8 inches long. Nail two of these pieces edgewise and crossways of frame one inch apart so that the hole is between them and equally distant from their ends. Cover these pieces with a strip of zinc two inches wide and eight inches long, and tack it on so that the edges of the zinc are flush with the outer edges of the wood strips. This forms an inlet for the cold air. Four inches on each side of the strip of zinc nail another strip of wood edgewise. These form a rest for the moisture pan. Place zincs and wood strips on the remaining holes in the same manner. From each projecting corner of the lower floor cut out a piece 3½ inches, square.

Cut two boards 10 inches wide and 2 feet 11½ inches long, and one board 10 inches wide and 4 feet 9 inches long. The shorter boards are to be nailed to the ends of the ventilator frame with the lower edges 1½ inches below the upper edge of the frame and the front end flush with the front board of the frame. The longest board forms the back and is to be nailed between the ends behind and next to the frame. Cut out ⅞ inche sufficient to let the upper edges of the 10 inch board be even. Drive nails so they will not be in the open space which forms the egg chamber; otherwise they will interfere with the egg drawers. These three boards form the ends and back of the egg chamber.

Make six pieces for sides of the egg drawers ⅜ inch by 1⅞ inch by 2 feet 8 inches long, also six pieces for ends ½ inch by 1⅞ inches by 17¾ inches long. Bore a ½ inch hole ¾ inch from the lower edge of the center of each of the end pieces. Saw a piece out from the lower edge up to the hole ½ inch wide. This forms a slot for the turning hook. Put pieces together by nailing the side pieces on the ends. Make twenty-four pieces ⅜ inch by 1⅞ inch by 2 feet 8 inches long. Champer (take off corner) the upper edges to ½ inch on upper surface ⅛ inch on edge. Six of these pieces are to be champered on one edge only. Nail eight of these pieces on the bottom of the frames with the champered edges up; the outside strips being those with one champered edge. In nailing these strips on make the spaces between them equal. These champered edges being set in this manner form a coping in which the egg is made to roll. Make up the three drawers in this way using 1 inch brads. Make another rack, to go inside of this frame, 2 feet 4½ inches long by 17¾ inches wide of ½ inch square pieces, with side pieces nailed onto end pieces. Set edgewise in this frame thirteen cross bars each ¼ inch by ⅜ inch with 1⅜ inch space between them. Before putting frame together lay off and cut out the slots to receive these crossbars. Set the bars so their upper edges will be level with the upper edge of the frame. This is for the purpose of turning the eggs and for this a screw eye is fastened in each end opposite the slot in the outer frame and is worked by means of a hook. This rack will have 2½ inch space to move in and will thus completely turn the egg. After putting the rack in place secure it by two small blocks on each side leaving a little play between blocks and rack.

Put the egg drawers in place and mark places for the dividing boards. For this purpose make two boards 6⅞ inches wide by 2 feet 8¼ inches long. Before putting in place nail a half inch square strip on each side on a line that will support and make the drawers run level. Have these boards fit down on the paper neatly. It will be found necessary to cut a piece out of each lower corner. The upper edges form a support for the hot water tank. Secure these dividing boards by nailing through the back board of the egg chamber. They had better be further secured by small corner blocks at the back corners and lower front corners, being careful to avoid interfering with the action of the drawer.

Make four blocks 1 inch square and 5 inches long. Place one in each corner of the egg chamber resting on the slides on which the drawers run. These are to support the tank while securing it in place, and also gives the correct space for the egg chamber. For the frame that supports the tank make two pieces 5¾ inches by 4 feet 9 inches, and two pieces 5¾ inchs by 2 feet 65⁄8 inches. Put these together by nailing the sides on the ends. One end will come in contact with the pipes. Before nailing get the exact size of the pieces to be cut out. and cut from the lower edge of the board. After fitting it neatly secure it to its place. Set the tank in its place and fasten by nailing through the flange with a few small nails: Have the tank and frame rest on the 5 inch block previously mentioned. In doing this it will be necessary to cut pieces from the 10 inch board to receive the pipes. The tank frame will pass inside of the 10 inch boards that form the egg chamber, and rest on the blocks. After the tank is properly fitted and leveled, nail it securely to place. Avoid puncturing the tank with nails. You are now ready to mark and put on the legs. These are to be made of two parts, the upper or square part that is fastened to the body and the lower or rounded part that forms the support. These are fastened together by a wooden pin being made with the lower part, and the hole in which it fits neatly in the upper part. The object of making them in this way is to enable the cabinet to be passed through any ordinary doorway, by taking off the lower part of the legs. Make the upper part 3½ inches square and 15 inches long. From the lower end of this part measure off 2¾ inches on one side. Saw in ⅞ inch and down from the top, taking out a piece ⅞ inch thick and 12¼ inches long. Do so with each of these pieces.

Set these blocks in corners that have been sawed out, letting the 10 inch board rest on shoulder. Nail these securely to their respective places.

Make a piece 3¾ inches wide and 5 feet 4 inches long and nail to front of egg chamber having the lower edge even with the bottom of lower floor. Cut two pieces 3 inchs wide and 65⁄8 inches long and fasten one on each end of front by letting it rest on end of the long board just put on. Make the upper piece the same length as lower one and 5¼ inches wide. Set this on the end pieces and fasten to the tank frame and upper part of the leg. These pieces form the frame for the glass doors that open into the egg chamber. Make three frames and fit with glass to fill this opening, one for each chamber. Hinge at the bottom, and have them small enough to leave a space of ⅛ inch at top. While the hatching is going on these frames swell.

We are now ready to put on the outside work. For the ends cut flooring boards 3 feet 5⁄8 inch long. For the back cut three boards 5 feet 55⁄8 inches long. First put on the end boards making them flush with each corner. Then put on the back boards. Nail these securely. Make a door for front 14½ inces wide and 5

feet long.   Hinge this on its lower edge even
with the lower floor.   When open it will per-
mit the chamber doors to open.   This door had
better be made with end pieces to prevent
warping.   Make two pieces 2¾ inches wide
and 14⅝ inches long and fasten on the front
corners and at the end of the door.   Make one
piece 5 inches wide and 5 feet 5½ inches long
and nail along the front and above the door.
The space between this outside case and the
egg chamber is to be filled with sawdust firmly
packed, and in case sawdust cannot be had use
bran.   To prevent this packing from spreading
the back out put in a block midway between the
ends with its upper end as high as the 10 inch
board.   Lay a sheet of building paper over the
machine with edges flush with outside casing.
To cover this top cut eight flooring boards 5
feet 7¾ inches long.   This allows one inch projection all around.   In putting this top on be
careful to have the hole for the inlet pipe properly located.   Under the projection put a ⅞ inch
molding.   If desired the top can first be put together with strips and fastened to the case with
screws.   In case it is desirable to remove it,
this way of making it will be found more convenient.   Make four strips to fit in corners.

Make a frame 18 inches by 18 inches outside measurement of 1 inch by 4 inch lumber. Toe-nail this on top of machine about center. Make a cover for this box same size as inside measure and nail cleats on inside, making the lid sit flush with upper edges of box. Put cleats on lid to prevent warping. Bore five holes 1¼ inch in the lid for ventilation. A molding may be put around the bottom of box. This box is known as the nursery.

Make the lamp box 5½ inches by 6¼ inches inside, and have the back 8 inches wide and extending upward 6¾ inches from the lower end of box. Leave the front open. Shape the side pieces same as shown in cut, and have them 14 inches high. Fasten this box on the end of the machine under the center of the large pipe so that the back comes up against under-side of machine, and nail securely. Make an extra bottom ⅞ inch thick with handle to place under lamp to hold it up to place.

This machine should be well painted, and in this respect the artistic eye can exercise its fancy.

How to make the Hot Air Brooder.

Cut six legs 2x2 and 21 inches long. Leave 7 inches at the upper end of these square and taper the balance of the distance down to 1 inch square at the lower end. Make the frame of 1 inch by 6 inch lumber. Cut two pieces of this frame 3 feet long and two pieces 2 feet 5½ inches long. Put these together by nailing the long pieces on the short ones. Put a leg in each corner of this frame, having the upper end of the leg flush with the upper edge of the frame. Put a bottom in this frame making the outside boards project 1 inch at one end. This projection receives the back end of another frame that stands in front and joining this one. Bore a 3 inch hole in the frame on the side that receives the lamp box, as shown in the cut. The lower edge of the hole must be 1½ inch from the lower edge of the floor. In each side piece of this frame bore two ⅜ inch holes; each hole ½ inch from upper edge and 3 inches from

the outside corner of the frame. The lamp box
must be made with care. Cut two boards for
the sides 8 inches wide, 19 inches on one edge
and 18 inches on the other edge. Cut two
boards 8 inches square, one for lamp seat and
the other to go above the lamp and forms the
bottom of the earth box. Bore a three inch
hole in the center of the upper bottom to receive
the hot air pipe. Fasten the upper bottom
with its lower edge 12½ inches above the lower edge of the box. Enclose the front of the
earth box with a board 4¾ inches wide. Put a
back on the lamp box extending from the lower
edge 13 inches high. Nail cleats on the bottom
of box as slides for the lamp seat. Make a door
to fit on front reenforcing it with cleats to prevent the heat from warping it. Bore a 3 inch
hole in the center of door and counter sink a
glass on outside. This is to be done so the
lamp can be seen from without. Bore five holes
in the back, five in the front in the door and
seven on each side of lamp box, close to the
lower edge of earth box. Make the holes
¾ inch and have them on a line. Cover these
holes on the inside with pieces of zinc 4 inches
wide and resting on ⅞ inch strips. Have one
of the longer edges fitted close up to the earth

box. This is done to let the gas and hot air escape and render the lamp safe to use out of doors. Bore twelve holes each ½ inch in lamp seat, three on each side and 1 inch from edge.

Place thimble in side of frame and put heating pipe in place. Fasten lamp box to side of brooder as shown in cut and nail firmly from inside of heating box. Fasten the stool band to floor of heating box. Put the 2 foot square shield with center over end of pipe, and its edges parallel to the sides of box. Fasten the feet to the floor of the box. Cover this heating box with a floor letting it project 2½ inches on each side, and 3 inches on the back end. Support the projecting edges with blocks which had better be put in place first. The boards for this floor must be cut 3 feet 3 inches long. The floor does not project over the front end that receives the other section of the brooder. Around the three sides of this floor nail a board 4¼ inches wide and ½ inch thick, leaving the front open.

Make a frame for the front section on feeding box the same size as the heating box frame Put two legs in front corners and let the other end rest on the projecting boards of the lower floor of heating box. Put a floor on this frame leaving the sides project the same as upper floor of heating box.   Cut two one inch boards 3 feet long with one end 12 inches wide and the other 7 inch wide.   Nail these boards on the side of this floor with straight edges flush with the lower edge of floor.   Put a board in the back or higher end of this box, having the upper edge flush with the 12 inch corners.   This board must be 7 inches wide, thus leaving a 4 inch space as a pass way from brooder to feed box. Put in a front board 7 inches wide, first cutting a small door in the under edge 4 inches by 20 inches and hanging it on the upper edge of opening.   Add the necessary fixtures to control it.   Over this box and on the higher end nail a board 12 inches wide and three feet 2 inches long.   To this board is hinged the sash lid as shown in cut.   Make this lid 2 feet 1 inch by 3 feet 2 inches with a center piece to support two panes of glass.

For the runway cut two pieces 1 inch by 2 inchs by 3½ feet long.   Cut the ends of these pieces so they will fit against the feed box and on the ground.   Cut enough ½ inch boards 2 feet 7 inches long to cover these pieces crossways.   Nail boards on having the ends flush with the outer edge.   On the upper surface of

these boards nail ½ inch strips running the same
direction as the boards, and 2½ inches apart.
Bore two holes on each side to receive the
standards of the sideboards, letting the holes
pass through floor and through the 2 inch pieces.
Make side boards and put on as shown in cut.
Fasten the three sections together with 3 inch
screen door hooks. We have yet to make the
top for the brooder. The roof of this top is
made with an under floor over which is the tin
roof with a space between the two. First cut
two pieces for rafters 3 feet 2 inches long 1½,
inch at each end and 2 inches in center, and
one piece for the third rafter of ½ inch lumber
the same length, 4½ inches at the ends and 4¾
inches at center. Cut two pieces of ½ inch
lumber 4½ inches wide and 3 feet 4½ inches
long for side pieces, nail these pieces with an
end of each on the ends of the widest rafter.
Put one of the other rafters half way and the
third one at the other end with the upper edges
of rafters in line and flush with side boards.
The floor of ½ inch lumber goes on the under
side of these rafters and to support the end at
the wide rafter it will be necessary to nail a strip
to that rafter, and then nail the floor to the strip.
There must be a short leg in each corner of

this floor for support. On the end that has the wide rafter bore a ¾ inch hole in each corner 4 inches from the end and 4 inches from each side. In each of the other corners bore similar holes 4 inches from sides and 1½ inch from end. Nail a block over each hole and bore holes through these blocks to give a better support to the legs. The legs must be 4 inches long with 1¼ inch pin to fit the hole. Nail them in place. Fill in above this floor with sawdust even with the top of the rafters and cover with a tin roof nailing the same around the edges and across the middle rafter with three penny fine nails. Cover the under or smooth side of this bottom with two thicknesses of cotton batting and this again by one thickness of canton flannel with the cotton side out. Nail these down with 4 oz tacks. Bring edges out flush with outside edges of legs and fit it neatly around the legs. Cut enough canton flannel 6 inches wide to go once around and 4 times the longway of the bottom. Fold the cloth with the cotton surface out and cut in from edges every 3 inches and within ½ inch of the fold. Open the fold and tack the cloth to place by putting the tacks through the crease. The four pieces for the center should divide the space equally. Tack every 3 inches opposite the cut. After having thus finished this top set it over the hot air chamber with the legs standing inside of the three sideboards, and is left moveable so the brooder can be cleaned. Above the end that fit against the feed box nail a tin gutter to drain off the rain.

In case it is desirable to apply heat to the feeding box an extra floor can be built under it and filled in with sawdust, or a second lamp and lamp box can be applied in the same manner as the one used with the brooder box.

If desirable to use a hot water brooder instead of a hot air brooder the foregoing described machine can be easily converted into such by making a water tank to fit in the hot air chamber and fit a lamp box under the center. The tank is to be the same length and width as box and 3 inches deep, and the floor over it of ½ inch lumber. Have the funnel shaped inlet and the faucet outlet conveniently placed in the back end. The lamp box must be 10 inches square on the inside and 15½ inches long. On a line 1½ inch from upper end bore 28 holes ¾ inch size, with eight of them on each side and six holes each on back and front. Cover these holes on the inside with zinc 4 inches wide tacked on ¾ inch strips. Have the ends

of the zinc meet and their upper edges flush
with the upper end of the box.   The lamp seat
must sit on cleats fastened to the lower edge
of box, and be movable.   In this seat bore 12
holes 1 inch from the edges and three of them
on each side.   Put door on with hinges and
means of fastening.   In the center of door cut
a 3 inch hole and countersink a glass on the
outside.   Cut a place in center of floor the size
of lamp box so that when the box is put in place
the end will be flush with the upper surface of
the floor and the tank will rest on it.

How to Make a Combined Incubator and Brooder House.

Dig a basement north and south suitably located 8½ by 10½ feet and 4½ feet deep. In making the frame use 2x4 inch lumber unless otherwise mentioned. For the mud sills frame four pieces, making the outside measures 8 feet by 10 feet. Have the roof slant to the south. Make the north corners 14 feet high and the south corners 12 feet high. Set two studding on the east and on the west sides dividing the space equally. On the north and south sides set two studdings in each, so the joists that are to be nailed to them will be 3 feet apart in the clear. Put in joists north and south using 2 inch by 6 inch pieces. Gain in the ribbon board on studding so the lower edge of the joist will be 6½ feet from the bottom of the basement. Put in two headers at the north end of the joist that are 3 feet apart, so as to form the walls of a hot air chamber 3 feet by 4 feet. This is for the brooder. Close the under side of this box with flooring. Bore a ⅜ inch hole in each corner as near the upper edge of the joist as possible. This is done to draw the heat to the upper floor, and to the corners of the brooder. Bore a 3 inch hole in one of the joists that forms the side of this box, with its center 2 feet from either end of the box and the lower edge of the hole 1½ inch from the lower edge of the floor. Make a lamp box for the brooder. Cut two boards 8 inches by 8 inches, one for under the lamp and the other for above it. Bore a 3 inch hole in the center of the upper one, for the heating pipe to come down through to meet the lamp flue. Measure up 12½ inches from the bottom of the lamp box to nail the upper bottom in. Nail the back on crossways. This will be 12½ inches high from lower end of box. Put a cap on the front crossways 6½ inches wide. Fasten the zinc thimble in the 3 inch hole of brooder chamber for the heating pipe to pass through. This is necessary to make it fire proof. Put in heating pipe and bring lamp box up to place and fasten by nailing to the joist. Now fill the box above the lamp and around the pipe with earth, to make the brooder fire proof. This box needs no door. Nail cleats on lower end of box for lamp shelf to slide on. Set a 2 foot square shield with its feet resting on floor of hot air chamber and its center over the mouth of the pipe, and its edges parallel with the sides of the chamber. The purpose of this shield is to scatter the hot air towards the sides of the chamber. Lay the floor of the room and at the same time mark on the floor the exact location of the hot air chamber. Make the brooder top by first making a frame 3 feet by 4 feet of 1 inch by 4 inch boards. Put on the inside of each corner a leg 8 inches long letting the top come flush with the upper edge of frame. Put a solid bottom in this frame with flooring cut 4 feet long, smooth side down. Cover the under or smooth side of this bottom with two thicknesses of cotton batting and this again by one thickness of canton flannel with the cotton side out. Nail these down with 4 oz. tacks. Bring edges out flush with the outside edges of legs and fit it neatly around legs. Cut enough canton flannel 6 inches wide to go once around and four times the long way of the bottom. Fold the cloth with the cotton surface out and cut in from edges every 3 inches and within a ½ inch of the fold. Open the fold and tack the cloth to place by putting the tacks through the crease. The four pieces for the center should divide the space equally. Tack every 3 inches opposite the cut. Put a No. 5 screw eye in the top of each corner post. In each eye fasten a rope. Bring ropes together and fasten, thereby forming a fastening for a rope to be used in raising and lowering the top. Pass this rope through a small pully in the roof directly over the center of air chamber, and down to the side of the room. Secure the rope to a small windlass or other convenient means by which the brooder top may be raised or lowered. Fill the top or frame with sawdust. Cover with light strips to keep the chickens from scratching it out. Put the outside or sheeting on beginning at the bottom. It is not necessary to nail the lower boards, but instead pack dirt behind as the boards are put in. As soon as you can get at the boards to nail them do so. Finish the outside up to a line with the floor. The south side is to be filled with glass beginning 1 foot above the floor line and extending 3 feet high and across the end of the building. Fit glass frames in the center of the east and west sides one foot above floor line, 3 feet by 4 feet. Finish sheeting the entire building

making a doorway on one side into the basement between the middle studding. Fit a door
neatly to this place. Make a door into the
upper room, on the same side as the lower
door, but near the south corner. Put on the
roof. On the south side and in the board
under the center of the glass frame cut a small
door 6 inches by 8 inches. This is to let the
chickens out and in. The chicken yard should
be 8 feet wide and at least 32 feet long. As a
fence for this yard, first fix a base board around
it 1 foot wide and to the upper edge of this nail
on 2 foot laths 1½ inch apart.

The incubator should sit in the basement on
the south side of the building, and will assist,
when in use, in keeping the building comfortable.

This building is large enough to accommodate
the No. 1 incubator. If desirable to keep the
incubator in operation it will be best to set the
brooder to one side and build in another one,
separating them by a partition fence. Also have
a partition fence extend through the center of
the yard. By making the building two feet wid-
er it will accommodate two No. 2 incubators.

The foregoing description gives the essential
parts in the construction of this building. As to
how it shall be finished I leave with the builder.

He may, as it pleases him, add window casings, weatherboarding, ceiling, filling spaces with saw-dust; painting, ventilating, preserving the under-ground lumber as per recipe, some of which are essential to comfort and others to the neatness and good appearance. If made thoroughly com-fortable you may rest assured it will do the work of hatching and raising chickens in the coldest weather if properly attended. The house is well adapted to the business for which it is built, and whoever undertakes the building of it may feel confident that it will do him good service, and the investment will be returned to him in a short time.

Those interested in the raising of chickens will readily see the advantage of building such a one as described in preference to any out-door brooder. This building affords protection dur-ing stormy weather. During bad days the chick-ens want freedom, exercise and food, as well as on good days, when they can be in the yard to obtain them. In this house they can have all of these and have none of the unpleasant features of bad weather. At the season of the year when this business is the most profitable, is the time protection must be had from bad weather. The out-door brooder of whatever manufacture does not afford this and at the same time give the chickens the desired room. It is these requirements that has developed the combined house and brooder, and of which I take pride in presenting to the readers of this little book. Any one taking the pains to investigate will find that the upper half of this house will not cost any more than the ordinary out door brooder and in addition it affords a room 8 feet by 10 feet which is much more desirable for the health and comfort of the chickens, and the convenience of handling them.

How to Build a Chicken House.

The following description is of a chicken house twice the size of the one shown in the cut. This building has been thoroughly tested and I have never found an arrangement that has equalled this for health, comfort and good results in the quantity of eggs received. The main building is 8 feet wide by 16 feet long, with roof slanting to the north; and outside walls and roof in good weather-proof condition. Make the north wall and both ends of 2 inch by 6 inch studding, with north wall 5 feet high. In the rest of the frame use 2 inch by 4 inch studding. The south wall should be 7 feet high. The ends and north side should be boarded up inside. First put on an 8 inch board and fill this space in with mortar and rock. The rest of the space is to be filled with sawdust. If built in this manner the rats cannot get up into the sawdust from below. The under side of the rafters should be ceiled and filled in the same manner. In putting on the roof leave places for ventilator pipes on the lower edge. A ventilator is required in the center of every 8 feet, and located on the north side. These ventilators should be made 4 inches square in the clear, and should begin 10 inches from the floor and extend 2 feet above the highest point of the roof. Along the north side of this room arrange the perches by putting a knee or bent every 5 feet, having them 20 inches high and extending 4 feet from north side of room. On these lay four pieces 1 by 4 inches the entire length of room. This will accommodate 150 chickens, the capacity of this house. It will be found convenient to put under this perch a floor slanting to the south as shown in the cut for convenience of cleaning. The object of thus arranging this perch is the convenience for chickens getting on and off, and the protection from severely cold weather by keeping them close together. Large and heavy chickens have trouble getting on and off high perches, and are often injured in doing so.

The nests are arranged on the south side of this room. Leave 2 feet at one end for the doorway. The bracket for supporting the nests should be 2 feet high and project 20 inches from the studding. Make the nest boxes for this building in two sections for the convenience of cleaning them. The bottom of the nest boxes should be a board 12 inches wide, and the nests divided by partition boards making the boxes 10 inches by 12 inches. The partition board should be 18 inches high at the back and slanting to 10 inches at the front. On the front of these nail a 4 inch board, letting it rest on the brackets. Cover the nests with a board which should have its upper surface perfectly smooth to prevent the chickens from resting on the boxes. An opening will be left in the front of each box 7 inches by 10 inches as an entrance. Nail a 6 inch board on the brackets flush with their front ends as a runway. Next, build a shed 10 feet wide, on the south side, the entire length of this building and adjoining it, as shown in the cut. The south side should be 5 feet and the rafters should join the main building 6 feet from the sill. Have the door in one end near the door that enters the main building. Board up both ends, leaving a place in each for a window about 2 feet by 3 feet. The south side should be boarded up 2 feet high and the remaining distance be fitted the entire length of building with movable glass frames.

In summer these frames can be taken out and the opening fitted with screens, thereby rendering the building more comfortable. Ceil the roof on the under side and fill in with saw-dust. Cover with corrugated board roofing and batten the joints. Protect this roof at once with a good coat of paint. Put boards on the south side of the partition wall, and have the lower one hinged on its upper edge, in sections of 8 feet the entire length of the building. Have a similar door on a line with the nest boxes, 6 inches wide for the convenience of gathering the eggs. In boarding up the space above the rafters, put in a small window 2 feet by 10 inches opposite each ventilator. On the south side of this room there should be a dust bath box 3 feet by 4 feet and 8 inches deep. Have one for every 8 feet of the length of the building. The yards can be any size suitable to the surroundings, and the fences of whatever material desirable.

There are several objects obtained in a building constructed in this manner. The chickens are best protected from inclement weather. No matter how uncomfortable it may be out of doors, the chickens are comfortaly housed in this building and at the same time are avoiding the disagreeable features of having to stay during a bad day in the same room in which they roost. Much comfort is gained both in winter and in summer by having the rafters ceiled and filled in with sawdust. While it is essential to protect from inclement weather it is also necessary to have good light and good ventilation for the best health of the chickens. More heat can be gained from the sun by having the south wall stand out at the bottom so the glass can receive the rays of the sun more directly. This will be an advantage in winter.

As to the manner in which the building shall be finished is a matter of choice with the builder. Weatherboarding, roofing, door casings, window casings, painting and foundation are features that are subject to the liking and means of the builder.

HOT WATER TANK.

Building Material Bills.

LUMBER FOR NO. 1 INCUBATOR.

8 pieces flooring 1 inch by 6 inches, 16 feet long.
1 piece popular board 1 inch by 10 inches, 12 feet long.
1 "   "   " 1 " " 16 " 16 " "
1 "   "   " 3⅜ " " 12 " 16 " "
1 "   4 inch by 4 inch 12 feet long for legs.

LUMBER FOR NO. 1 BROODER.

2 boards 1 inch by 12 inch 12 feet long, finished hard pine.
5 pieces flooring 1 inch by 6 inch 16 feet long.
4 lath.   1 piece 2 inch by 4 inch, 12 feet long.

LUMBER FOR INCUBATOR AND BROODER HOUSE.

10 pieces 2 inches by 4 inches, by 12 feet.
8 " 2 " " 4 " " 14 "
2 " 2 " " 4 " " 16 "
2 " 2 " " 4 " " 10 "
1 piece 1 inch " 4 " " 8 "
1 " 1 " " 4 " " 14 "
1 " 1 " " 6 " " 16 "
4 pieces 2 " " 6 " " 10 "
1 piece 2 " " 6 " " 6 "

500 feet stock boards ; 100 feet roofing boards ; 110 feet flooring 1 inch by 6 inches, 16 feet. Batting sufficient to cover
cracks of the roof.

LUMBER FOR CHICKEN HOUSE 8 BY 16 FEET WITH SHED 10 FEET WIDE.

8 pieces 2 inches by 4 inches by 10 feet.

5	"	2	"	"	4	"	"	12	"
2	"	2	"	"	4	"	"	14	"
5	"	2	"	"	4	"	"	16	"
2	"	2	"	"	4	"	"	18	"
2	"	2	"	"	6	"	"	16	"
2	"	2	"	"	6	"	"	10	"
5	"	1	"	"	4	"	"	16	"
3	"	1	"	"	6	"	"	16	"
2	"	1	"	"	12	"	"	14	"
1	piece	1	"	"	16	"	"	14	"
1	"	1	"	"	12	"	"	16	"
1	"	2	"	"	4	"	"	20	"

For roofing. 10 feet boards 160 feet ; 12 feet boards 176 feet. For siding, 400 feet.

TIN FOR INCUBATOR NO. 1.

A tank 2 feet $6\frac{1}{2}$ inches wide by 4 feet $6\frac{1}{4}$ inches long by $5\frac{3}{4}$ inches deep with $\frac{3}{4}$ inch flange on upper edge all around. On the bottom inside and crossways have 3 ribs 1 inch high dividing the space equally. These brace the bottom and form supports for the pipes. Have the coil of pipes made as shown in the cut. The center pipe is $2\frac{1}{2}$ inches and the smaller ones $1\frac{1}{4}$ inches. The large pipe outside is 4 inches and is continuous with the sides of the tank. The $2\frac{1}{2}$ inch pipe comes down through the center of the 4 inch pipe and the space between the two is closed at the lower end. This allows the water to come down to the lamp. In the $2\frac{1}{2}$ inch pipe where it forms the "T" with the cross pipe of same size at the farther end, put a piece of tin so the current of hot air will be divided equally. The upper ends of elbows on small pipes should be a $\frac{3}{8}$ inch free opening. After the pipes are properly fitted put on a top over all and solder it. Leave an opening $1\frac{3}{4}$ inches near one corner for the inlet pipe. This pipe is 4 inches long with $\frac{3}{4}$ inch opening, with screw top and a flange just below the top 1 inch wide and is fastened in the wood top that goes over the tank. The large elbow is 7½ inches from throat to tank and 2½ inches from throat to lower end. Fit the 2½ inch pipe so that it is in the center of the 4 inch pipe and their lower ends even. The small elbows stand 7½ inches out from tank. The faucet and connection is at the lower edge and at one corner, and is 6¾ inches from tank to the cut-off. Have 6 pipes ¾ inch opening 2¼ inches long with a flange ¾ inch on one end. Also 6 galvanized iron 8 inches by 12 inches by ¾ inch deep; also 6 strips of zinc 2 inches by 8 inches.

TIN FOR BROODER IN BROODER HOUSE.

A square piece of sheet iron 2 feet each way, with ¼ inch edge turned up. Have a 4 inch support rivited on each corner with the end turned for a foot so that the sheet will stand 4 inches from the floor. A 2½ inch elbow pipe, one end 18 inches from throat to end and the other 2½ inches from throat to end. A zinc thimble 3 inches in diameter and 2 inches long to go in heating box for hot air pipes to go through. Put a flange ¾ inch wide on short end ¾ inch from the edge to keep dirt from falling on the lamp. On the long end of pipe fit a stool band so it will support the pipe, keeping it ¾ inches from floor.

The same parts are required in the out-door hot air brooder, with the addition of sufficient tin to cover the roof 3 feet ¾ inch wide and 2 feet 11½ inches long. Turn up ½ inch that goes up against the feed box. A strip of tin 3 feet 1 inch long and 3 inches wide broke in center lengthways to form an eave trough and is tacked on the back end of feed box over the line where the brooder joins it.

For the hot water brooder there will have to be in addition to the above a tank 2½ feet by 2½ feet by 3 inches deep of galvanized iron with top soldered on. The inlet pipe must be elbow shaped and 1¼ inch size, 7½ inches from throat to the tank, the other 1 inch, or long enough to receive a screw top. The outlet at the lower edge of tank and 4 inches from tank to the cut-off. Both to be situated in the same end of tank. This is for the No. 1 brooder.

The lamp best suited for these incubators and brooders is a plain glass fount with handle standing 4 inches high from bottom to top of brass collar. Use an alabastine plain top flue, and the best No. burner.

SUPPLIES AND PARTS.

In case you cannot get all the parts required conveniently I will furnish them delivered at the depot here properly packed for shipping at the following prices:

Egg drawer...$	.40
Rack for drawer.....................................	.40
Egg drawer and rack...............................	.75
Outside door, panneled............................	.75
Corner strips, per set of 4........................	.40
Legs, per set of 4..................................	1.00
Lamp box and lamp seat...........................	.40
Nursery box...	.50
Tank for No. 1......................................	10.00
Tank for No. 2......................................	8.00
Tank for No. 3......................................	5.50
Tank for No. 4......................................	3.25
Lamps complete.....................................	.50
Thermometer (tested).............................	.75

SUPPLIES FOR BROODER.

Lamp box..$	.75
Shield...	.30
Heahing pipe, complete.............................	.35

How to Care for an Incubator.

The lamp should be well cared for and kept in good condition never allowing it to become blackened or smoked. Before putting in the eggs set the machine to working two or three days, and bring the temperature up to the required degree, and be sure you have everything fixed to hold it at that point. Attend the incubator regularly. Do not open the egg drawer any oftener than is required. Do not let the moisture pans go dry. When the chicks are breaking through the shell do not open egg drawer oftener than once in six hours. The incubator should be in a quiet place free from noises particularly those that jar and cause things to vibrate, and free from draughts. A basement or cellar that is free from dampness is the preferable location. Wherever it sits have it protected from any cold air while in operation and particularly when the egg drawer

is open.   Have the tank filled to 5½ inches of
boiling water.   No. 1 incubator takes about 25
gallons, No. 2 about 16 gallons, No. 3 about 10
gallons and No. 4 about 5 gallons.   Set the
lamp to burning and see that you can keep the
temperature at 103 degrees.   The first three or
four days a temperature of 102 degrees will do,
but then get it up to 103 degrees.   The temperature should not vary more than four degrees
either way.   In cold weather if you have any
trouble in keeping the temperature up to the
required degree, draw off two or three gallons,
reheat it and put it back again.

From the 18th day until the chicks come off
keep the temperature at 104 degrees.   Care
should be taken not to let it get over 104 degrees
for any length of time, as over heating causes
deformed chicks.   Care should be taken not to
jar the eggs.

Place all the eggs on their sides lengthwise
between the bars of the moveable racks and at
the same time let the egg lie in the groove of
lower frame so that as the rack is moved it
causes the egg to roll back and forth on its side.
Place the thermometer between the two front
rows of eggs so you can see the temperature
through the glass door.   Place the bulb of the

thermometer half way down between the eggs, so you get the right temperature at the center of the egg. The thermometer should lie so that the top end will be about two inches higher than the bulb.

The turning of the eggs is done by the use of a wire hook without opening the inside door. place the hook through the hole in door and and drawer into the eyelet in the turning rack; the eggs are rolled back or forth by moving this rack 2½ inches either way. Commence turning the second day, turn twice daily the first five days, after the fifth day turn four times daily up to the 16th day, after that twice until the hatch is over. Divide the time for turning as near equally as you can.

From the fifth day until the hatch is coming off take the egg drawers out with their contents once each day and let the eggs cool down to 80 degrees. Replace them and at the same time turn the drawers end for end, and turn the eggs. It is preferable to cool them in the evening. While cooling leave the egg chambers open for ventilation.

On the fifth day put in half of the moisture pans ⅔ filled with warm water and ¼ inch of clean sand in the bottom of each pan. On the twelfth day put in the remaining pans filled in the same manner.   On the 16th day empty all the pans of water and refill with fresh warm water. Try the eggs the 14th day and see if they are moist enough.   You do this by taking some of the eggs out of different parts of the machine, and placing them in warm water about 100 degrees temperature.   15 or 20 eggs will be plenty to try.   If they sink they are too moist; if they float high they are too dry; if they float showing enough of the egg out of the water which can be covered by a twenty-five cent silver piece they are just right.   This will be the average only, as some will show more and others less; less rather than more.   This is a reliable test in all cases, as anyone can prove by trying.   If the eggs float as stated, and a poor hatch results, the trouble must be looked for elsewhere.   It will usually be found with the temperature.   If you find the eggs too moist on the 14th day, take the moisture pans out for two or three days, then put them back again; and if you find the eggs too day on the 14th day, place a wet sponge in each end of the egg drawer.   If these sponges get dry in twenty-four hours, saturate them again and replace. If they do not lose any more of their moisture, they are not needed any longer.

In dry weather you need more moisture than you do in wet weather; also in a dry room or dry cellar you will need more moisture than in a damp cellar.

When the chicks begin to come out keep the incubator closed for six hours, then take the chicks that are free from the shell and place in the drying box on top of the incubator in flannel that should be placed there a few days before, so as to be warm. When the chicks are nicely dry, put them in the brooder. Give them their first feed when they are 24 hours old, and their drink when 36 hours old.

Fill and trim the lamp every 12 hours. Keep the burner clean. See that the lamp is all right each night.

We certainly prefer the brooder to hens for several reasons, the principal one being the ease and facility with which a large number of chicks can be attended to. Then brooder chicks have no lice or mites about them, and none are killed, as hens kill them with their clumsy feet.

Some Causes for Chicks Dying in the Shell in the Incubator.

There are many causes why chicks die in the shell, and some of them are due to the management of the incubator and others are found in other sources. I will note a few of them and if the operator of an incubator has trouble of this kind he will in all probability find the cause among them.

Improper ventilation, too much moisture, over-heating, running with too low a temperature, bad air in cellar or room in which the incubator is sitting, too much dampness in the egg chamber; too dry an air in the egg chamber, especially from the 16th day till the hatch comes off, old eggs, over-fed breeding stock; inbred stock, or from any cause in which the egg has lost its vitality or fertility.

Select good eggs, such as you would put under a hen. The incubator cannot do more than the hen, but can make a better success if properly attended.

What Shall I Build?

The best thing that I can recommend my readers as an aid in the poultry business is the combined incubator and brooder house. . The raising of chickens is of sufficient importance to give it a separate building especially fitted and adapted for that purpose. In this building you have the incubator and brooder, both of which are essential, conveniently located to the advantage of each other, and are free from the annoyances that attend when they are used separately, and taking up room that you need for something else. The expense is light and the returns will soon satisfy the investment. If any accident should happen to your lamp endangering the safety of things, it is separated where its damage will be limited. The chickens can have all desired advantages under any conditions of weather, and can best be protected from the piratical inclinations of such animals that consider the tender chicken a sweet morsel created for their especial purpose,

Protect the Weak Ones.

Keep chicks of the same age separated from others. This is essential to the successful raising of chickens. They need to be separated as a matter of protection from the abuse inflicted by older ones, also from the piratical inclinations of the older ones. The chicks must have their quantity of food, if they would thrive, and it is essential they should enjoy their feed undisturbed and unharmed. Very often chickens of the same age are weakly and they should be protected in the same manner. The weakly ones should have special advantages in feeding, of which they can not be deprived. In this way they will soon become strong and able to take care of themselves without special attention. In feeding corn chop always scald it. When fed dry it will swell in the crop and it thus often kills them. Never feed on the ground but on a board, and see that the board is cleaned before feeding.

Inbreeding.

There is nothing that will depreciate the health and quality of poultry as that of allowing them to inbreed. The successful stockraiser appreciates this fact and zealously guards against it, spending money and using all the time and taking all the trouble necessary to continually bring new life blood in the herd. One of the most successful ways of getting new blood into the flock is to get, from a reliable breeder a setting of eggs of your own choice. Another way is to get a good healthy male bird and put with the hens. Use whatever means at your command, but be sure this is accomplished every year. The best time of the year to bring new blood into the flock is in the fall. At that time you get the best of the flock before they are sold off and can usually get them cheaper. There should be a male bird with every dozen hens, and if it is desired to keep the kind of breed distinct they should be kept in separate apartments.   Inbreeding impoverishes the flock, lays them more liable to disease, and subjects them to all of the troubles that come to the poultry yard.

When new and strange birds are brought in they had better be quarantined for a few days, until you ascertain their freedom from disease or vermin.   It is alweys advisable to dust them with insect powder.   In case there are those that have scaly legs, they must be kept apart until doctored, as it is a trouble that communicates to others. Rub each day with ointment made of equal parts of kerosene oil and lard.

Health in Poultry.

When fowls are judiciously fed and made to take exercise, their quarters kept clean and free from vermin there will be but little chance for disease to get in its work. It is a lack in these things that bring on nearly all of the troubles with poultry. Poultrymen should know the causes of diseases in poultry, and it will be traceable in nearly every case to a neglect in the eatables given them. When the combs and wattles are of a bright red, it indicates a good condition of health. On entering the hennery at night, if no wheezing sounds can be heard you can rest assured there are no roupy fowls in the flock. The digestive organs indicate a good healthy condition when the droppings are hard and portions of it white. When the edges of the combs and wattles are purplish red, and their movements sluggish the keeper had better see to the feed or look for vermin, or guard against cholera. It demands attention, and with diligence he will find the cause. When fowls lie around indifferent to their surroundings and show a healthy condition they are too fat and they are liable to die of apoplexy, indigestion or liver complaint, and should be compelled to shift for themselves in order that digestion may become more active.

Diseases and their Treatment.

ROUP.

This disease in chickens corresponds to distemper in horses. The symptoms in its first stages are as follows: A wheezing sound and running at the nostrils. As the disease advances the head and eyes become swollen, the mouth becomes cankered, and they refuse to eat. Cases have been noted in which the eyes became so swollen that they burst from their sockets. This is regarded as the most dreaded disease among poultry and is the poutryman's worst enemy. A bad cold is the forerunner of roup. Improper ventilation and letting the flock out too early in the morning are two causes of them taking cold. Close watching is necessary to guard against this disease. A cold can be cured without much trouble, but roup is difficult to handle and harder to get rid of. Be constantly on your guard against it.

As soon as you see the chickens are taking cold, make a smoke in the poultry house in the evening after they have gone to roost of equal parts of pine tar and sulphur. Go in yourself while smoking them, so you will not suffocate them. They can stand as much of the smoke as you can. If they do get the roup separate the diseased ones. It is contagious and the rest of the poultry must be protected. Treat the diseased ones according to the receipe for the cure of roup found in the back part of this book.

CHOLERA.

After the farmer and poultryman more thoroughly understands the diseases of poultry they will come to the conclusion that a majority of the cases of reported cholera are not such, but are troubles caused by lice and indigestion, and is caused be eating such seeds as hard grains of corn without sufficient grit to thoroughly masticate them. I have always made it a rule to furnish plenty of gravel for my poultry of all ages, or a mortar of lime and sand broken up after drying. The chickens are fond of grits, requiring surprising quantities at an early age, and thrive the better by having, it especially if they are confined. Furnish plenty to them at the start if you would have them grow fast. By furnishing a good supply of grits for the poultry yard it not only avoids cholera, but many other diseases. Examine the gizzard of a healthy fowl and it will be found to contain a good supply of gravel and other grits. There should be in the gizzard more grit than food. Should there be more food than grit found it would show a congested and unhealthy condition of the gizzard and an inability for this organ to perform its proper function. In a diseased condition there will sometimes be found no grit whatever but a stale mass of undivided food. This shows inability of the organs to do their work, and such results are for want of plenty of grit in the gizzard. As a result of these conditions there will follow indigestion, diseased bowels and liver, and unless soon relieved death will follow, and for the want of knowledge as to the true facts we through our ignorance pronounce it cholera. Do not understand me to imply that the use of grit will prevent these diseases, as they may be produced from other causes. I am thoroughly convinced that a free use of grit will keep the fowls in such a healthy and vigorous condition that disease will find no place in which to entrench itself. Especially prepared grits are of late abundantly found in the market and are superior to gravel, and should find a place in every poultry house by the side of oyster shells, bones, etc., and such like. Fowls are very fond of these prepared grits.

The symptoms of cholera are as follows:— Loss of vigor, showing decided weakness, combs turn purple, eyes are dim, stagger as they walk, the droppings are thin and green. They rarely live longer than thirty-six hours.

The remedy for this disease will be found among the recipes in the latter part of this book.

APOPLEXY OR INDIGESTION.

This disease is caused from over-feeding and a failure to get the required exercise. The chickens lie around indifferent to the usual sounds, yet look healthy, and, in fact, are in excellent condition. Indigestion and inactive liver follow, and they die. The remedy is to feed in limited quantities and force them to hunt and scratch more.

VERMIN AND SORE THROAT.

When poultry is infected with lice they are restless and constantly picking in their feathers.

In young poultry, especially ducklings, the throat becomes swollen and swallowing is difficult. Remedy for this will be found in recipe in latter part of this book.

Some Causes of Poultry Diseases.

———

Filthy houses produce lice.
Jumping from high roosts—bumble foot.
Draughts and dampness in hennery—roup.
Impure water, lice and inbreeding—cholera.
Damp quarters—diarrhea.
Musty food—canker.
Inbreeding—consumption.
Over-feeding—apoplexy.
Unwholesome diet—indigestion.
· Close confinement—debility.
Want of exercise—feather and egg eating.
Exposure to cold and dampness—rheumatism.
High feeding—leg weakness.
Birds with large combs must not be allowed out of doors during severe weather, if it is intended to have them lay well during winter. A frozen comb is a notice to quit laying. Plastered walls in the hen house not only keep out cold in winter but do not offer hiding places for vermin. A double purpose is thus gained.

Kitchen Cabinet.

The following description is of my Kitchen Cabinet, and will be found to possess the handiest arrangement for use in the kitchen that has ever been gotten up. Its price, delivered free on board cars at Arkansas City, Kansas, is $10. Should any one wish to make it themselves the following description will be found sufficient to enable them to do so.

The legs are 2½ by 2½ inches by 2 feet 5 inches long; the square part is 9½ inches. The front ⅞ by 6 inches wide and 3 feet 3⅝ inches between shoulders. End rail ⅞ by 6 inches by 1 foot 11 inches long, between shoulders. Top 2 feet 7 inches by 4 feet long. Back 20½ inches high by 4 feet long. Bread board 18¾ by 24 inches. Flour bins 2 feet long by 9½ inches deep, rounded as shown in cut, by 19½ inches wide, or front measure. Face of drawer 2½ inches wide. The end strip for slide ⅞ by 3½ inches, with groove ½ by ¼ inch. Center strip for drawer slides ⅞ by 6½ inches wide, with ½ inch hard wood nailed and glued on bottom edge.   The large drawer is 18¼ inches wide by 2 feet long by 3½ inches deep.   Top of cabinet 8 inches by 4 feet.   Cover table with a zinc 2 ft. 7 inches wide by four 4 ft. long.   The edge of wood top is coped out so the zinc can be neatly nailed.   After drawers are made for flour bins, cover the bottom with tin.   Make cabinet case with drawers as shown in the cut. Also finish up back in same way.

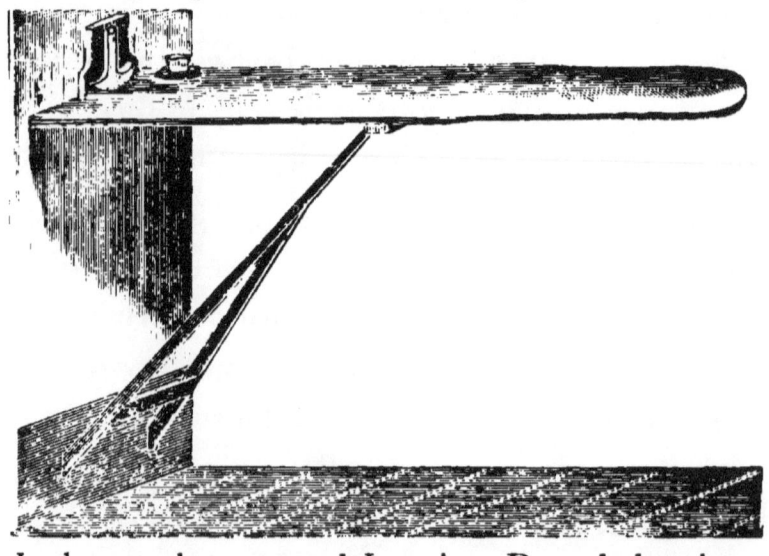

I also make a good Ironing Board that is convenient, substantial and durable.   The cut explains all that need be.   It speaks for itself. The price of this board is $2; or I will deliver, free on board cars at Arkansas City, Kansas, the brace stick and fixtures for $1.

Recipes.

AN EXCELLENT WHITEWASH.

This whitewash is an excellent one for the poultry houses and fences, and will not rub off, lasting almost as well as ordinary paint.

It is prepared in the following manner: Slack ½ bushel of lime in boiling water, rain water is preferred; strain this so as to remove all sediment; add 2 ℔ sulphate of zinc; 1 ℔ common salt; ½℔ of whiting. Mix to the proper consistency with skim milk and apply while hot. If white is not desired, add coloring to suit.

Those who have tried this formula consider it good. For use around the poultry house many prefer it to paint because it cleanses and purifies the surroundings as well as adding to their appearance. This should be applied twice a year.

A GOOD FEED TO MAKE HENS LAY IN WINTER.— A MORNING FEED FOR FIFTY HENS.

Two quarts corn chop, two quarts oat chop, two quarts good wheat bran; take one pint of cracklings, put them in a pan and put enough water in to moisten thoroughly; let this come to a boil, then pour it over the feed and stir till all is moistened, and feed warm in a trough. Add one quart of oil meal to this feed. An occasional use of a little red or cayenne pepper is sometimes recommended. Be sure and put a good handful of salt in this feed every time. Never let your chickens of any age have any water until they have eaten their morning feed. Care should be taken not to give the feed too hot. Thirty minutes after they have eaten their morning feed small grain of some kind should be thrown in the straw to give them exercise in the forenoon, this litter should be changed twice a week, sweep the floor every time you change the litter.

The noon feed should be wheat, millet or oats. This should be scattered in straw or a litter of some kind, thus giving them exercise in cold weather. Their evening feed should be hard parched corn, and feed it good and warm. For a change boil small potatoes and some beets, turnips or carrots and cooked apples; this makes a good feed for them occasionally. They should have some greens every day in winter. It is a good plan to sow some wheat or rye near the poultry buildings for the hens to range on, or in worst weather you can give them raw cabbage or turnips. Gravel, lime and charcoal should always be in their reach. Ground bone meal and such grits as the markets afford are good. Get some of them at least.

A GOOD TONIC TO KEEP YOUR HENS IN GOOD HEALTH.

Sulphate of iron, 1 lb; sulphuric acid, 2 ounces; water, 1 gallon; mix and dissolve. Dose: Shake well and give one tablespoonful to one quart of water. Give this twice a week in the drinking water. I am not troubled with diseases of any kind in my flock, as I use preventatives all the time. Be sure and whitewash the poultry house twice a year. Scatter slacked lime around in every corner and all over the floor once a month, and oil the perches once a month with a cheap grade of coal oil.

THE FIRST FEED FOR LITTLE CHICKS.

Break an egg and beat the white and yellow together. Fry or bake it in a pan—not brown, but just so it is done. Rub it fine with your fingers and feed them with it the first few days every two hours; but the last feed in the evening should be oat meal or millet seed for the first two weeks. After the third day feed with bread made of two quarts of corn meal, one quart of wheat or graham flour and middlings, one pint of oat meal, half a teacup of ground fresh meat and 3 eggs and one teaspoonful of baking soda; the whole mixed into a stiff dough and baked two hours in an oven. This, when cold, is crumbled and fed every three hours for the first two weeks.

Then take one quart of wheat bran, one quart of corn chop, one pint middlings, and one table-spoonful of salt; stir all together and scald it. Be careful not to get it too wet. Put a little oil meal in this feed twice a week.

Be sure and keep plenty of fresh water before the chicks all the time, and keep plenty of millet seed and small wheat, charcoal and bone meal or other grits before them all the time after the first week. Give them some greens every day. Boiled millet seed makes a nice feed for big or little chickens.

If you go according to this bill you will be all right for getting chicks ready for the market in eight or nine weeks. Be sure and keep plenty of gravel or sand and lime before your chicks from the beginning. A chicken 8 weeks old should weigh from 1 lb to 1 ½ lbs.

A SURE CURE FOR ROUP.

Willow charcoal, 3 drachms; powdered ginger, 4 drachms; capsicum, 3 drachms; powdered rhubarb, 3 drachms; powdered chalk, 1 ½ ounces; gum camphor, 1 drachm; assafoetida, 4 drachms.

Take one pint of fine corn meal and dry thoroughly in the baker and mix half of this recipe in the pint of meal. This is for 150 fowls. Let the fowls get real hungry, put this in pans and set in different parts of the house; as they eat it they will inhale the odor. If they refuse to eat it gather it all up, and after they are all on the perches go in and shut the door and sow it broadcast over the flock; this will cause them to sneeze. With two or three applications of this kind you will have no more roup.

How to prevent roup.—Always have your poultry house well ventilated and never let any draught draw over your flock.

GERMAN CHOLERA RECIPE.

Assafoedtida, 1 ounce; ginger, 1 tablespoonful; gentian, 1 tablespoonful; black antimony, 1 tablespoonful; red pepper, 1 tablespoonful; carbonate of iron 1 tablespoonful. Mix all together thoroughly. When required for use make into pills with linseed oil.

Dose.—Give from one to two pills morning and evening, as the case may be, until the fowl is cured

ANOTHER CHOLERA RECIPE.

A simple and effective cure is gained by confining the diseased fowls and feeding them cane seed, and fresh water.

LICE.

To rid a hen house of lice, close up all ventilators and doors. Now take an old iron pot put some red hot coals in it and set it in the her

house.   Now take ½ ℔ of rosin, 2 ounces of
carbolic acid, mix with 1℔ of sulphur and ½℔
of smoking tobacco, wrap these ingredients in a
paper, drop them in the pot on the red hot coals,
come out quickly and close the door, leave the
house closed until it is done smoking.   Now
whitewash once a month.   To three gallons of
whitewash use two quarts of salt and half box of
concentrated lye.   Whitwash house, nests and
perches and once a week wash the perches with
cheap coal oil and you will have no trouble with
lice.   If you are troubled with mites, disolve ½
box of Lewis lye in 2 gallons of hot soapsuds.
Now take a broom or white wash brush and
wash the poultry house thoroughly on the inside,
perches and all, with the lye water for two or
three mornings in succession, and where you
can not get with the brush pour some of the lye
water in.   This preparation is death to anything, be careful to keep it out of the reach of
children

Remember one thing, a hen cannot be a successful egg machine so long as she has to raise
lice.   Furthermore no treatment will cure a sick
fowl as long as lice or mites are allowed to sap
her vitality.   If desirable to rid the fowls quickly of lice and mites make a solution of 2 oz. car-

bolic acid to a gallon of water. Take the bird by the bill and feet and dip it by drawing it backwards through this solution but once. Keep its eyes out of the liquid.

Tobacco stems hung in different parts of the poultry house is a preventitive of lice and mites.

DEATH TO LICE.

Put ½ ℔ of black sulphur and ½ ℔ of air slacked lime in the dust box, this will keep them off and give them a glossy appearance.

HOW TO BREAK UP A SETTING HEN.

The desire to incubate comes on as soon as each series of eggs is layed. As soon as this desire comes on her, she should be confined in comfortable and roomy quarters and be furnished plenty of water and stimulating food. She will in a short time go to laying again, and thus profitably engage the time that would otherwise be wasted, and herself made a burden to her keeper.

RECIPE FOR A GOOD REFRESHING DRINK.

Take 4 ℔s of brown sugar, put into 3 pints of

water and boil till the scum rises, then skim it
and set it off to cool. Dissolve ⅛lb of Tartaric acid in one pint of cold water. Take 2
tablespoonfuls of Jamaica ginger, tie in a thin
cloth and drop in a pint of boiling water and
boil ten minutes.' Take the whites of six fresh
eggs and beat to a fine frost. Dissolve a large
teaspoonful of soda in a quart of cold water.
When all is cold, stir together and flavor with 3
teaspoonfuls of lemon essence, and put in a jug
or bottle and cork tight and it will not spoil.
When wishing to use, shake well and take 3
tablespoonfuls to 1 pint of ice water.

MOCK APPLE PIE.

2 cups of bread and cracker crumbs.
1 cup of sugar.
1 teaspoon level full of tartaric acid.
1 teaspoonful of cinnamon.
3 teacups of water.
Mix all together and divide into three pies.
The above recipe will make a pie that can
scarcely be told from one made of green apples.

DIRECTIONS TO MAKE A GOOD BABY FOOD.

Take one pint of wheat flour and tie in a piece
of cheese cloth that has been washed and drop

in a pot of boiling water and boil one hour, then take it out of the cloth and peal the outside off and throw it away, now scrape or grate the balance and put in a glass jar for use.   Keep the lid on the jar.   To prepare for use for a baby under 3 months old, take a level teaspoonful of the food and put into a half-pint of cold water with a little pinch of salt and set it on the stove and stir until it comes to a boil, now pour this in a pint of fresh sweet milk with one teaspoonful of granulated sugar, and set in boiling water and boil 15 minutes, then put in a cold place and just warm enough at a time for each feed.   This amount will last about 12 hours, as it must be made fresh every 12 hours.   As the child gets older you add more food and more milk.   Feed in a nursing bottle and rinse the bottle every time it is used and clean it out with soda every morning.   Be sure and give the baby cold water at any age, as they need it to be healthy.

THE BEST LINIMENT OUT FOR MAN AND BEAST.

Turpentine, ½ gallon; gum camphor, 4 oz.; mix and let stand until dissolved, then add carbolic acid, 4 oz., and pure petroleum ½ gallon; then mix all together and it is ready for use.

Always shake well before using. The petroleum is the best lubricating oil of West Virginia. This liniment will cure the worst case of sweeny on a horse by applying warm.

A SURE CURE FOR CABBAGE WORMS.

Take a sprinkler and sprinkle the cabbage with hot water from 150 to 160 degrees. Begin as soon as the worms make their appearance. Two or three sprinklings during the season will be sufficient. Water at this temperature will not injure the cabbage but will destroy the worms. Be sure and keep the water at that degree of heat. Use a thermometer to test the water with.

TO PRESERVE POSTS.

Take boiled linseed oil and stir in it pulverized charcoal to the consistency of paint, put a coat of this over the timber and there is not a man that will live to see it rot.

FURNITURE POLISH.

1 pint of alchohol, 1 oz. of shellac, 1 1/4 oz. copal, 1 oz. dragon's blood, mix and dissolve, apply with sponge or soft brush.

A GOOD CHEAP LINIMENT.

Boil equal parts of linseed oil and turpentine.

IMPERIAL WASHING FLUID.

1 can Lewis' concentrated lye, 1 oz. of salts of tartar, 2 oz. of spirits of ammonia to a gallon of rainwater. Dissolve one can of the lye, when cold add salts of tartar and ammonia. Half a teacup full of this fluid to a boiler full of clothes, shaving the ordinary amount of soap.

A SURE CURE FOR FISTULA WITHOUT CUTTING IT OUT.

Take 1 oz. of sweet oil, 1 oz. spirits of turpentine, 1 oz. alcohol, 1 oz. Hartshorn, 1 oz. sasafras oil, 1 oz. oil ganian, 1 oz. cedar oil, 1 oz. spike. Mix these well, put in bottle and keep well corked. Shake well before using.

Take hogs lard and grease around the part effected by the fistula. Pour some of the liniment on until the effected part is well saturated. Take a piece of old carpet and hold on the diseased part, and on this hold a hot smoothing iron until the horse flinches. This healing is done to blister the parts. In 24 hours after the liniment and heat are applied, take a small blade of an ordinary pocket knife and puncture the blister by entering it at one side and let the blade pass under the skin, but not deep into the flesh. Now take as much calomel as will lie on the large blade of the ordinary pocket knife, roll it in some cotton and pass it into the cut made in the blister. After putting the calomel in grease around the cut with lard about twice a week. If properly cared for it will not leave a a scar. This remedy is simple and effective. It has been thoroughly tested; it has proved a success.

A SURE CURE FOR SPLINT AND BONE SPAVIN.

Take 1 oz. sweet oil, 1 oz. spirits of turpentine and 2 oz. creosote, mix and shake well before using. Use this twice a day as a liniment. Use lard around the outside of the parts effected to protect the hair.

A SURE CURE FOR DIARRHEA IN YOUNG CALVES.

Tie 2 quarts of wheat flour in a thin sack and drop in boiling water and boil one hour, then peal the outside off and scrape ½ pint of the flour into 2 quarts of sweet milk, then make it warm enough for the calf to drink, give this twice a day until the calf is well. In a very bad case you can add ½ teaspoonful of the essence of jamacia ginger to each feed.

DIRECTIONS TO MAKE A GOOD POWDER FOR SORES ON HORSE AND MAN

Get 5 cents worth of alum and put it on a hot stove and leave it there until it quits boiling, then take off and let cool, then pulverize to a fine powder. To use it, wash the sores with castile soap and dust the powder on plentifully while the sore is wet and it will heal the worst sore shoulder in a few days.

HOW TO SET AN EVERGREEN TREE.

Dig your pits plenty large so you can spread the roots out straight and set the tree about 2 inches deeper than it was, cover the bottom of the pits with small rock, then 2 inches of rich soil, a bucket of water, then the tree. Now cov- the roots with rich soil and tamp it good; now another bucket of water and another layer of rock and a layer of earth. Rock and earth till you get to the top, and you will never loose a tree.

I trust that every one ordering this book will use the information it contains to their own advantage. Should your neighbor see the ground you have gained in its use let him send and get one for himself. You will confer a fovor by impressing upon him its value and thereby do him good and at the same time oblige the author.

Sent to any address postage paid on receipt of $1.00

JACOB YOST,
Arkansas City, Kansas.

INDEX.

www.ingramcontent.com/pod-product-compliance
Lightning Source LLC
Chambersburg PA
CBHW020032030726
47499CB00007B/2387